THE COUNTRY OF THE COMERS- BACK

BY

LAFCADIO HEARN

Copyright © 2013 Read Books Ltd.
This book is copyright and may not be
reproduced or copied in any way without
the express permission of the publisher in writing

British Library Cataloguing-in-Publication Data
A catalogue record for this book is available from the
British Library

CONTENTS

LAFCADIO HEARN 1

THE COUNTRY OF THE COMERS-BACK 3

LAFCADIO HEARN

Patrick Lafcadio Hearn was born in Lefkada, Greece in 1850. He was baptized in the Greek Orthodox Church, but in his infancy, his family relocated to Dublin, Ireland, where Hearn attended the Roman Catholic Ushaw College. Neither of these religious faiths stuck, however, and when he was nineteen Hearn went to the United States, where he began to work in journalism. He gained employment as a reporter for the *Cincinnati Daily Enquirer* in 1872, and became known as an investigative yet sensational journalist.

In 1877, Hearn left Cincinnati for New Orleans, where he remained for almost a decade. His writings about the city's unique cultural life, especially its creole population and distinctive cuisine, were published in magazines such as *Harper's Weekly* and *Scribner's Magazine*. His best-known New Orleans works are *Gombo Zhèbes, Little Dictionary of Creole Proverbs in Six Dialects* (1885), *La Cuisine Créole* (1885), and *Chita: A Memory of Last Island*, a novella first published in *Harper's Monthly* in 1888. Over the decade, Hearn became a much-loved chronicler of the city; today, more books have been written about him than any former resident of New Orleans other than Louis Armstrong.

Between 1887 and 1890, Hearn worked as a correspondent

in the West Indies, before settling in Japan, a country that would provide his greatest inspiration. At a time when Japan was largely unknown to Westerners, Hearn became world-famous for his writings on the country. His book *Glimpses of Unfamiliar Japan* (1894) was hugely popular, and in 1896 he began teaching English literature at Tokyo Imperial University. Hearn penned three more books concerned with Japan and Japanese culture. Amongst the best-remembered of these are his collections of Japanese ghost stories and legends, such as *Japanese Fairy Tales* (1898) and *Kwaidan: Stories and Studies of Strange Things* (1903). Kearn died in Tokyo, Japan in 1904, aged 54. His grave is at the Zōshigaya Cemetery in Toshima, Tokyo.

THE COUNTRY OF THE COMERS-BACK

Lafcadio Hearn

Night in all countries brings with it vaguenesses and illusions which terrify certain imaginations – but in the tropics it produces effects peculiarly impressive and peculiarly sinister. Shapes of vegetation that startle even while the sun shines upon them assume, after his setting, a grimness, – a grotesquery, – a suggestiveness for which there is no name. . . . In the North a tree is simply a tree; – here it is a personality that makes itself felt; it has a vague physiognomy, an indefinable *Me;* it is an Individual (with a capital 'I'); it is a Being (with a capital 'B').

From the highwoods, as the moon mounts, fantastic darknesses descend into the roads – black distortions, mockeries, bad dreams, – an endless procession of goblins. Least startling are the shadows flung down by the various forms of palm, because instantly recognisable; – yet these take the semblance of giant fingers opening and closing over the way, or a black crawling of unutterable spiders. . . .

Nevertheless, these phasma seldom alarm the solitary and belated Bitaco: the darknesses that creep stealthily along the path have no frightful signification for him, – do not appeal to his imagination; – if he suddenly starts and stops and stares, it is not because of such shapes, but because he has perceived two specks of orange light, and is not yet sure whether they are only fire-flies, or the eyes of a trigonocephalus. The spectres of his fancy have nothing in common with those indistinct and monstrous umbrages: what he most fears, next to the deadly serpent, are human witchcrafts. A white rag, an old bone lying in the path, might be a *maléfice* which, if trodden upon, would cause his leg to blacken and swell up to the size of an elephant's limb; an unopened bundle of plantain leaves or of bamboo strippings, dropped by the way-side, might contain the skin of a *Soucouyan*. But the ghastly being who doffs or dons his skin at will – and the zombi – and the *Moun-Mò* – may be quelled or exorcised by prayer; and the lights of shrines, the white gleaming of crosses, continually remind the traveller of his duty to the Powers that save. All along the way there are shrines at intervals, not very far apart: while standing in the radiance of one niche-lamp, you may perhaps discern the glow of the next, if the road be level and straight. They are almost everywhere, – shining along the skirts of the woods, at the entrance of ravines, by the verges of precipices; – there is a cross even upon the summit of the loftiest peak in the island. And the nightwalker removes his hat each time his bare feet touch the soft stream of yellow light outpoured from the illuminated shrine of a white Virgin or a white Christ. These are good ghostly company for him; – he salutes them, talks to them, tells them his pains or fears: their blanched faces seem to him full of sympathy; – they appear to cheer him voicelessly as he strides from gloom to gloom, under the goblinry of those woods which tower black as ebony under the stars. . . . And he has other companionship. One of the greatest terrors of darkness in other lands does not exist here after the setting of the sun – the terror of *Silence*. . . . Tropical night is full of voices – extraordinary populations of crickets are trilling; nations of tree-frogs are chanting; the *Cabri-des-bois** or *cracra*, almost deafens you with the wheezy bleating sound by which it earned its creole name; birds pipe: everything that bells, ululates, drones, clacks, guggles, joins the enormous chorus; and you fancy you see all the shadows vibrating to the force of this vocal storm. The true life of Nature in the tropics begins with the darkness, ends with the light.

And it is partly, perhaps, because of these conditions that the coming of the dawn does not dissipate all fears of the supernatural. *I ni pè zombi mênm gran'-jou* ('he is afraid of ghosts even in broad daylight') is a phrase which does not sound exaggerated in these latitudes, – not, at least, to anyone knowing something of the conditions of tropical day, in the hush of the woods, the solemn silence of the hills (broken only by torrent voices that cannot make themselves heard at night), even in the amazing luminosity, there is a something apparitional and weird, – something that seems to weigh upon the world like a measureless haunting. So still are all Nature's chambers that a loud utterance jars upon the ear brutally, like a burst of laughter in a sanctuary. With all its luxuriance of colour, with all its violence of light, this tropical day has its ghostliness and its ghosts. Among the people of colour there are many who believe that even at noon – when the boulevards behind the city are most deserted – the zombis will show themselves to solitary loiterers.

Here a doubt occurs to me, – a doubt regarding the precise nature of a word, which I call upon Adou to explain. Adou is the daughter of the kind old capresse from whom I rent my room in this little mountain cottage. The mother is almost precisely the colour of cinnamon; the daughter's complexion is brighter, – the ripe tint of an orange. . . . Adou tells me creole stories and *tim-tim*. Adou knows all about ghosts, and believes in them. So does Adou's extraordinarily tall brother, Yébé, – my guide among the mountains.

'Adou,' I ask, 'what is a zombi?'

The smile that showed Adou's beautiful white teeth has instantly disappeared; and she answers, very seriously, that

she has never seen a zombi, and does not want to see one.
'*Moin pa te janmain ouè zombi, – pa 'lè ouè ço main!*'
'But, Adou, child, I did not ask you whether you ever saw it; – I asked you only to tell me what it is like?'...
Adou hesitates a little, and answers:
'*Zombi? Mais ça fai désòde lanuitt, zombi!*'
'Ah! it is Something which "makes disorder at night."'
Still, that is not a satisfactory explanation. 'Is it the spectre of a dead person, Adou? Is it *one who comes back?*'
'*Non, Missié, – non; çé pa ça.*'
'*Not that?*... Then what was it you said the other night when you were afraid to pass the cemetery on an errand, – *ça ou té ka di*, Adou?'
'*Moin té ka di: "Moin pa lé k'allé bò cimétiè-là pa ouappò moun-mò; – moun-mò ké barré moin: moin pa sé pè vini enco."*' (I said, 'I do not want to go by that cemetery because of the dead folk; – the dead folk will bar the way, and I cannot get back again.')
'And you believe that, Adou?'
'Yes, that is what they say . . . And if you go into the cemetery at night you cannot come out again; the dead folk will stop you – *moun-mò ké barré ou*'....
'But are the dead folk zombis, Adou?'
'No; the *moun-mò* are not zombis. The zombis go everywhere: the dead folk remain in the graveyard....

Except on the Night of All Souls: then they go to the houses of their people everywhere.'

'Adou, if after the doors and windows were locked and barred you were to see entering your room in the middle of the night, a woman fourteen feet high?'...

'*Ah! pa pàlé ça!!*'...

'No; tell me, Adou.'

'Why, yes: that would be a zombi. It is the zombis who make all those noises at night one cannot understand.... Or, again, if I were to see a dog that high [she holds her hand about five feet above the floor] coming into our house at night, I would scream: *Mi Zombi!*'

Then it suddenly occurs to Adou that her mother knows something about zombis.

'*Ou! Maman!*'

'*Eti!*' answers old Théréza's voice from the little outbuilding where the evening meal is being prepared, over a charcoal furnace, in an earthen canari.

'*Missié-là ka mandé save ça yé yonne zombi; – vini ti bouin!*'... The mother laughs, abandons her canari, and comes in to tell me all she knows about the weird word.

'*I ni pè zombi*' – I find from old Théréza's explanations – is a phrase indefinite as our own vague expressions, 'afraid of ghosts', 'afraid of the dark'. But the word 'zombi' also has special strange meanings.... '*Ou passé nans grand chimin lanuitt, épi ou ka ouè gouôs difé, épi plis ou ka vini assou difé-à pli ou ka ouè difé-à ka màché: çé zombi ka fai ça. . . . Encò, chouval ka passé, – chouval ka ni anni toua patt: ça zombi.'* (You pass along the high-road at night, and you see a great fire, and the more you walk to get to it the more it moves away: it is the zombi makes that. . . . Or a horse with only three legs passes you: that is a zombi.)

'How big is the fire that the zombi makes?' I ask.

'It fills the whole road,' answers Théréza: '*li ka rempli toutt chimin-là*. Folk call those fires the Evil Fires, – *mauvai difé;* – and if you follow them they will lead you into chasms, – *ou ké tombé adans labîme*'.

And then she tells me this:

'Baidaux was a mad man of colour who used to live at St Pierre, in the Street of the Precipice. He was not dangerous, – never did any harm; – his sister used to take care of him. And what I am going to relate is true, – *çe zhistouè veritabe!*

'One day Baidaux said to his sister: "*Moin ni yonne yche, va! – ou pa connaitt li!*" (I have a child, ah! – you never saw it!) His sister paid no attention to what he said that day; but the next day he said it again, and the next, and the next, and every day after – so that his sister at last became much annoyed by it, and used to cry out: "*Ah! mais pé guiole ou, Baidaux! ou fou pou embêté moin conm ça! – ou bien foul!*". . . . But he tormented her that way for months and for years.

'One evening he went out, and only came home at midnight leading a child by the hand, – a black child he had found in the street; and he said to his sister: –

' "*Mi yche-là moin mené ba ou! Tou léjou moin té ka di ou moin tini yonne yche: ou pa té 'lè couè, – eh, ben! MI Y!*" ' (Look at the child I have brought you! Every day I have been telling you I had a child: you would not believe me, – very well, LOOK AT HIM!)

'The sister gave one look, and cried out: "*Baidaux, otí ou pouend yche-là?*" . . . For the child was growing taller and taller every moment. . . . And Baidaux, – because he was mad, – kept saying: "*Cé yche-moin! cé yche moin!*" (It is my child!)

'And the sister threw open the shutters and screamed to all the neighbours, – "*Sécou, sécou, sécou! Vini oué ça Baidaux mené ba moin!*" (Help! help! Come see what Baidaux has brought in here!) And the child said to Baidaux: "*Ou ni bonhè ou four!*" (You are lucky that you are mad!) . . . Then all the neighbours came running in; but they could not see anything: the zombi was gone.'

As I was saying, strange things happen in the hours of daylight here; – and it is of something which walks abroad under the eye of the sun, even at high noontide, that I wish to speak, while the impressions of a journey one morning to the scene of its last alleged appearance yet remain vivid

The Country of the Comers-Back

in my mind.

You follow the mountain road leading from Calebasse over long meadowed levels two thousand feet above the ocean, into the woods of La Couresse, where it begins to descend slowly, through deep green shadowing, by great zigzags. Then, at a turn, you find yourself unexpectedly looking down upon a planted valley, through plumey fronds of arborescent fern. The surface below seems almost like a lake of gold-green water, – especially when long breaths of mountain-wind set the miles of ripening cane a-ripple from verge to verge: the illusion is marred only by the road, fringed with young cocoa palms, which serpentines across the luminous plain. East, west, and north the horizon is almost wholly hidden by surging of hills: those nearest are softly shaped and exquisitely green; above them loftier undulations take hazier verdancy and darker shadows; farther yet rise silhouettes of blue or violet tone, with one beautiful breast-shaped peak thrusting up in the midst; – vapourous huddling of prodigious shapes – wrinkled, fissured, horned, fantastically tall. . . . Such at least are the colours of the morning. . . . Here and there, between gaps in the volcanic chain, the land hollows into gorges, slopes down into ravines; and the sea's vast disc of turquoise flames up through the interval. Southwardly those deep woods, through which the way winds down, shut in the view. . . . You do not see the plantation buildings till you have advanced some distance into the valley; – they are hidden by a fold of the land, and stand in a little hollow where the road turns; a great quadrangle of low grey antiquated edifices, heavily walled and buttressed, and roofed with red tiles. The court they form opens upon the main route by an immense archway. Farther along ajoupas begin to line the way, – the dwellings of the field hands, – tiny cottages built with trunks of the arborescent fern or with stems of bamboo, and thatched with cane-straw: each in a little garden planted with bananas, yams, couscous, camanioc, choux-caraibes, or other things, – and hedged about with roseaux d'Inde and various flowering shrubs.

Thereafter, only the high whispering wildernesses of cane on either side, – the white silent road winding between its swaying cocoa trees, – and the tips of hills that seem to glide on before you as you walk, and that take, with the deepening of the afternoon light, such amethystine colour as if they were going to become transparent.

It is a breezeless and cloudless noon. Under the dazzling downpour of light the hills seem to smoke blue: something like a thin yellow fog haloes the leagues of ripening cane, – a vast reflection. There is no stir in all the green mysterious front of the vine-veiled woods. The palms of the roads keep their heads quite still, as if listening. The canes do not utter a single susurration. Rarely is there such absolute stillness among them; upon the calmest days there are usually rustlings audible, thin cracklings, faint creepings: sounds that betray the passing of some little animal or reptile – a rat or a manicou, or a zanoli or couresse, – more often, however, no harmless lizard or snake, but the deadly *fer-delance*. Today, all these seem to sleep; and there are no workers among the cane to clear away the weeds – to uproot the *pié-treffe, piépoule, pié-balai, zhèbe-en-mè;* it is the hour of rest.

A woman is coming along the road, – young, very swarthy, very tall, and barefooted, and black-robed; she wears a high white turban with dark stripes, and a white foulard is thrown about her fine shoulders; she bears no burden, and walks very swiftly and noiselessly . . . Soundless as shadow the motion of all these naked-footed people is. On any quiet mountain-way, full of curves, where you fancy yourself alone, you may often be startled by something you *feel*, rather than hear, behind you, – surd steps, the springy movement of a long lithe body, dumb oscillations of raiment; – and ere you can turn to look, the haunter swiftly passes with creole greeting of '*bonjou*' or '*bonsouè, Missié.*' This sudden 'becoming aware' in broad daylight of a living presence unseen is even more disquieting than that sensation which, in absolute darkness, makes one halt all breathlessly before great solid objects, whose proximity has been revealed by some mute blind emanation of force alone. But it is very seldom, indeed, that the negro or half-breed is thus surprised: he seems to divine an advent by some specialised sense, – like an animal – and to become conscious of a look directed upon him from any distance or from behind any covert; – to pass within the range of his keen vision unnoticed is almost impossible. . . . And the approach of this woman has been already observed by the habitants of the ajoupas; – dark faces peer out from windows and doorways; – one half-nude labourer even strolls out to the road-side under the sun to watch her coming. He looks a moment, turns to the hut again, and calls: –

'*Ou-ou! Fafa!*'

'*Étï! Gabou!*'

'*Vini ti bouin! – mi bel négresse!*'

Out rushes Fafa, with his huge straw hat in his hand: '*Oti̇̈, Gabon?*'

'*Mi!*'

'*Ah! quimbé moin!*' cries black Fafa, enthusiastically; '*fouinq! li bel! – Jésis-Maïa! li doux!*' . . . Neither ever saw that woman before; and both feel as if they could watch her forever.

There is something superb in the port of a tall young mountain-griffone, or -negress, who is comely and knows that she is comely: it is a black poem of artless dignity, primitive grace, savage exultation of movement. . . . '*Ou marché tête enlai conm couresse qui ka passé larivie*' (You walk with your head in the air, like the couresse-serpent swimming a river) is a creole comparison which pictures perfectly the poise of her neck and chin. And in her walk there is also a serpentine elegance, a sinuous charm: the shoulders do not swing; the cambered torso seems immobile; – but alternately from waist to heel, and from heel to waist, with each long full stride, an indescribable undulation seems to pass; while the folds of her loose robe oscillate to right and left behind her, in perfect libration, with the free swaying of the hips. With us, only a finely trained dancer could attempt such a walk; – with the Martinique woman of colour it is natural as the tint of her skin; and this allurement of motion unrestrained is most marked in those who have never worn shoes, and are clad lightly as the women of antiquity, – in two very thin and simple garments; – chemise and *robe d' indienne*. . . . But whence is she? – of what canton? Not from Vauclin, nor from Lamentin, nor from Marigot, – from Case-Pilote or from Case-Navire: Fafa knows all the people there. Never of Sainte-Anne, nor of Sainte-Luce, nor of Sainte-Marie, nor of Diamant, nor of Gros-Morne, nor of Carbet, – the birthplace of Gabou. Neither is she of the village of the Abysms, which is in the Parish of the Preacher, – nor yet of Ducos nor of François, which are in the Commune of the Holy Ghost. . . .

She approaches the ajoupa: both men remove their big

straw hats; and both salute her with a simultaneous '*Bonjou, Manzell.*'

'*Bonjou, Missié,*' she responds, in a sonorous alto, without appearing to notice Gabou, – but smiling upon Fafa as she passes, with her great eyes turned full upon his face. . . . All the libertine blood of the man flames under that look; – he feels as if momentarily wrapped in a blaze of black lightning.

'*Ça ka fai moin pè,*' exclaims Gabou, turning his face towards the ajoupa. Something indefinable in the gaze of the stranger has terrified him.

'*Pa ka fai moin pè – fouing!*' (She does not make me afraid) laughs Fafa, boldly following her with a smiling swagger.

'*Fafa!*' cries Gabou, in alarm. '*Fafa, pa fai ça!*'

But Fafa does not heed. The strange woman has slackened her pace, as if inviting pursuit; – another moment and he is at her side.

* '*Oti ou ka rété, chè?*' he demands, with the boldness of one who knows himself a fine specimen of his race.

* '*Zaffai cabritt pa zoffai lapin,*' she answers, mockingly.

'*Mais pouki ou rhabillé toutt nouè conm ça.*'

'*Moin pòté deil pou name moin mò.*'

'*Aïe ya yaïe! . . . Non, vouè! – ca ou kallé atouèlement?*'

'*Lanmou pàti: moin pàti deïé lanmou.*'

'*Ho! – ou ni guêpe, anh?*'

The Country of the Comers-Back

'*Zanoli bail yon bal; épi maboya rentré ladans.*'
'*Di moin oti ou kallé, doudoux?*'
'*Jouq lariviè Lezà.*'
'*Fouinq! – ni plis passé trente kilomett!*'
'*Eh ben? – ess ou 'lè vini épi moin?*'*

And as she puts the question she stands still and gazes at him; – her voice is no longer mocking: it has taken another tone, – a tone soft as the long golden note of the little brown bird they call the *siffleur-de-montagne*, the mountain-whistler. . . . Yet Fafa hesitates. He hears the clear clang of the plantation bell recalling him to duty; – he sees far down the road – (*Ouill!* how fast they have been walking!) – a white and black speck in the sun: Gabou, uttering through his joined hollowed hands, as through a horn, the *ouklé*, the rally call. For an instant he thinks of the overseer's anger, – of the distance, – of the white road glaring in the dead heat: then he looks again into the black eyes of the strange woman, and answers: '*Oui; – moin ké vini épi ou.*'

With a burst of mischievous laughter, in which Fafa joins, she walks on, – Fafa striding at her side. . . . And Gabou, far off, watches them go, – and wonders that, for the first time since ever they worked together, his comrade failed to answer his *ouklé*.

17

'*Coumentyo ka crié ou, chè?*' asks Fafa, curious to know her name.

'*Châché nom moin ou-menm, duviné.*'

But Fafa never was a good guesser, – never could guess the simplest of tim-tim.

'*Ess Céndrine?*'
'*Non, çé pa ça.*'
'*Ess Vitaline?*'
'*Non, çé pa ça.*'
'*Ess Aza?*'
'*Non, çé pa ça.*'
'*Ess Nini?*'
'*Câché encò.*'
'*Ess Tité?*'
'*Ou pa save, – tant pis pou ou!*'
'*Ess Youma?*'
'*Pouki ou 'lè save nom moin? – ça ou ké fai épi y?*'
'*Ess Vaiya?*'
'*Non, çé pa y.*'
'*Ess Maiyotte?*'
'*Non! ou pa ké janmain trouvé y!*'
'*Ess Sounoune? – ess Loulouze?*'

She does not answer, but quickens her pace and begins

The Country of the Comers-Back

to sing, – not as the half-breed, but as the African sings, – commencing with a low long weird intonation that suddenly breaks into fractions of notes inexpressible, then rising all at once to a liquid purling bird-tone, and descending as abruptly again to the first deep quavering strain:

'*À tè –*
moin ka dòmi toute longue;
Yon paillasse sé fai moin bien,
Doudoux!
À tè –
moin ka dòmi toute longue;
   Yon robe biésé sé fai moin bien,
Doudoux!
À tè –
   moin ka dòmi toute longue;
Dè jolis foulà sè fai moin bien
Doudoux!
À tè –
   moin ka dòmi toute longue;
Yon joli madras sé fai moin bien,
Doudoux!
À tè –
   moin ka dòmi toute longue:
Cé à tè . . .'

Obliged from the first to lengthen his stride in order to keep up with her, Fafa has found his utmost powers of walking overtaxed, and has been left behind. Already his thin attire is saturated with sweat, his breathing is almost a panting; – yet the black bronze of his companion's skin shows no moisture; her rythmic step, her silent respiration, reveal no effort: she laughs at his desperate straining to remain by her side. '*Marché toujou' deié moin, – anh, chè? – marché toujou' deie!* . . .

And the involuntary laggard – utterly bewitched by the supple allurement of her motion, by the black flame of her gaze, by the savage melody of her chant – wonders more and more who she may be, while she waits for him with her mocking smile.

But Gabou – who has been following and watching from afar off, and sounding his fruitless *ouklé* betimes – suddenly starts, halts, turns, and hurries back, fearfully crossing himself at every step.

He has seen the sign by which She is known. . . .

None ever saw her by night. Her hour is the fullness of the sun's flood-tide; she comes in the dead hush and white flame of windless noons, – when colours appear to take a very unearthliness of intensity, – when even the flash of some colibri, bosomed with living fire, shooting hither and thither among the grenadilla blossoms, seems a spectral happening

The Country of the Comers-Back

because of the great green trance of the land. . . .

Mostly she haunts the mountain roads, winding from plantation to plantation, from hamlet to hamlet, – sometimes dominating huge sweeps of azure sea, sometimes shadowed by mornes deep-wooded to the sky. But close to the great towns she sometimes walks: she has been seen at midday upon the highway which overlooks the Cemetery of the Anchorage, behind the cathedral of St Pierre. . . . A black woman, simply clad, of lofty stature and strange beauty, silently standing in the light, *keeping her eyes fixed upon the Sun.* . . .

Day wanes. The further western altitudes shift their pearline grey to deep blue where the sky is yellowed up behind them; and in the darkening hollows of nearer mornes strange shadows gather with the changing of the light – dead indigoes, fuliginous purples, rubifications as of scoriac, – ancient volcanic colours momentarily resurrected by the illusive haze of evening. And the fallow of the canes takes a faint warm ruddy tinge. On certain far high slopes, as the sun lowers, they look like thin golden hairs against the glow, – blond down upon the skin of the living hills.

Still the woman and her follower walk together, – chatting loudly, laughing, chanting snatches of song betimes. And now the valley is well behind them; – they climb the steep road crossing the eastern peaks, – through woods that seem to stifle under burdening of creepers. The shadow of the woman and the shadow of the man, – broadening from their feet, – lengthening prodigiously, – sometimes mixing, fill all the way; sometimes, at a turn, rise up to climb the trees. Huge masses of frondage, catching the failing light, take strange fiery colour; – the sun's rim almost touches one violet hump in the western procession of volcanic silhouettes. . . .

* * *

Sunset, in the tropics, is vaster than sunrise. . . . The dawn, upflaming swiftly from the sea, has no heralding erubescence, no awful blossoming – as in the North: its fairest hues are fawn-colours, dove-tints, and yellows, – pale yellows as of old dead gold, in horizon and flood. But after the mighty heat of day has charged all the blue air with translucent vapour, colours become strangely changed, magnified, transcendentalised when the sun falls once more below the verge of visibility. Nearly an hour before his death, his light begins to turn tint; and all the horizon yellows to the colour of a lemon. Then this hue deepens, through tones of magnificence unspeakable, into orange; and the sea becomes lilac. Orange is the light of the world for a little space; and as the orb sinks, the indigo darkness comes – not descending, but rising, as if from the ground – all within a few minutes. And during those brief minutes peaks and mornes, purpling into richest velvety blackness, appear outlined against passions of fire that rise half-way to the zenith, – enormous furies of vermilion.

The Woman all at once leaves the main road, – begins to mount a steep narrow path leading up from it through the woods upon the left. But Fafa hesitates, – halts a moment to look back. He sees the sun's huge orange face sink down, – sees the weird procession of the peaks vesture themselves in blackness funereal, – sees the burning behind them crimson into awfulness; and a vague fear comes upon him as he looks again up the darkling path to the left. Whither is she now going?

'*Oti ou kallé là?*' he cries.

'*Mais conm ça! – chimin tala plis cou't, – coument?*'

It may be the shortest route, indeed; – but then, the *fer-de-lance!*. . . .

'*Ni sèpent ciya,   en pile.*'

No: there is not a single one, she avers; she has taken that path too often not to know:

'*Pa ni sèpent piess! Moin ni coutime passé là; – pa ni piess!*'

She leads the way. . . . Behind them the tremendous glow deepens; – before them the gloom. Enormous gnarled forms of ceiba, balata, acoma, stand dimly revealed as they pass; masses of viney drooping things take, by the failing light, a sanguine tone. For a little while Fafa can plainly discern the figure of the Woman before him; – then, as the path zig-zags into the shadow, he can descry only the white turban and the white foulard; – and then the boughs meet overhead: he can see her no more, and calls to her in alarm:-

'*Oti ou? – moin pa pè ouè arien.*'

Forked pending ends of creepers trail cold across his face. Huge fire-flies sparkle by, – like atoms of kindled charcoal blown by the wind.

'*Içitt! – quimbé lanmain-moin!*' . . .

How cold the hand that guides him! . . . She walks swiftly, surely, as one knowing the path by heart. It zig-zags once more; and the incandescent colour flames again between the trees; – the high vaulting of foliage fissures overhead, revealing the first stars. A *cabritt-bois* begins its chant. They reach the summit of the morne under the clear sky.

The wood is below their feet now; the path curves on eastward between a long swaying of ferns sable in the gloom, – as between a waving of prodigious black feathers. Through the further purpling, loftier altitudes dimly loom; and from some viewless depth, a dull vast rushing sound rises into the night . . . Is it the speech of hurrying waters, or only some tempest of insect voices from those ravines in which the night begins? . . .

Her face is in the darkness as she stands; Fafa's eyes are turned to the iron-crimson of the western sky. He still holds her hand, fondles it, murmurs something to her in undertones.

'*Ess ou ainmein moin conm ça?*' she replies, almost in a whisper.

Oh! yes, yes, yes! . . . more than any living being he loves her! . . . How much? Ever so much, – gouôs conm caze! . . . *Yet she seems to doubt him, – repeating her question over and over:* '*Ess ou ainmein moin?*'

And all the while – gently, caressingly, imperceptibly, – she draws him a little nearer to the side of the path, nearer to the black waving of the ferns, nearer to the great dull rushing sound that rises from beyond them: – "*Ess ou ainmein moin?*'

'*Oui, oui!*' he responds, – '*ou save ça! – oui, chè doudoux, ou save ça!!* . . .

And she, suddenly, – turning at once to him and to the last red light, the goblin horror of her face transformed, – shrieks with a burst of hideous laughter: – '*Atò bô!*' (Kiss me now!)

For the fraction of a moment he knows her name: – then, smitten to the brain with the sight of her, reels, recoils, and, backward falling, crashes two thousand feet down to his death upon the rocks of a mountain torrent.

* In creole, *cabritt-bois* ('the Wood-Kid') – a colossal cricket. Precisely at half-past four in the morning it becomes silent; and for thousands of early risers too poor to own a clock, the cessation of its song is the signal to get up.

  * 'Where are you staying, dear?'

  * 'Affairs of the goat are not affairs of the rabbit.'
'But why are you dressed all in black like this?'
'I wear mourning for my dead soul.'
'*Aïe ya yaïe!* . . . No, true! . . . where are you going now?'
'Love is gone: I go after love.'
'Ho! you have a Wasp (lover) – eh?'
'The zanoli gives a ball; the *maboya* enters unasked.'
'Tell me where you are going, sweetheart?'
'As far as the River of the Lizard.'
'*Fouinq!* – that is more than thirty kilometres!'
'What of that? – do you want to come with me?'

www.ingramcontent.com/pod-product-compliance
Ingram Content Group UK Ltd.
Pitfield, Milton Keynes, MK11 3LW, UK
UKHW041422180426
11947UKWH00007B/239